June 2, 2018

Baby Martin,

    I can't wait to meet you!

        love Grandma Martin

HAT ON, HAT OFF

by **Theo Heras**

Illustrations by Award-winning Artist
Renné Benoit

pajamapress

Time to go out!
Need a hat

Hats in basket
Red hat, green hat,
striped hat

Which hat?

Hat on

Hide that itchy sweater

Hat off

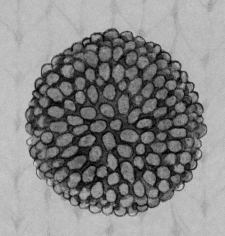

Left shoe, right shoe

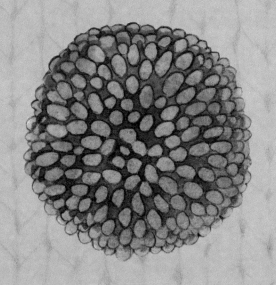

Tie up tight

One sleeve, two sleeves

Button up jacket

Hat on

Hat off

Need sippy cup
And pail and shovel

Hat on

Potty?

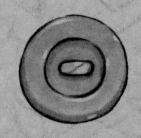

Flush
Pull up pants

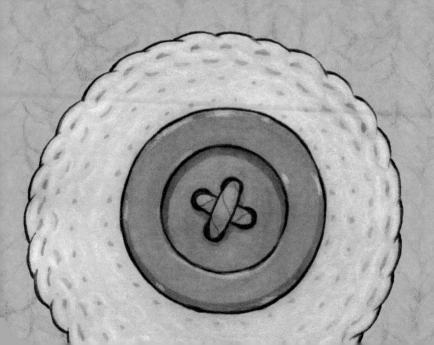

Hat off

Hat on

Wait!

Where is Bunny?

Hat off

Here is Bunny

Bunny wears his hat

Hat On

Away in stroller

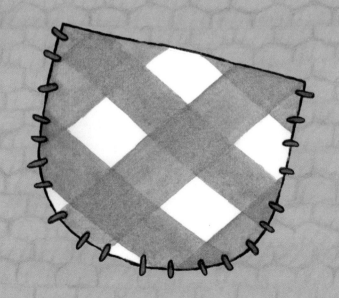

Hat Off

First published in the United States and Canada in 2016

Text copyright © 2016 Theo Heras
Illustration copyright © 2016 Renné Benoit
This edition copyright © 2016 Pajama Press Inc.
This is a first edition.

10 9 8 7 6 5 4 3 2 1

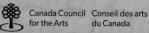

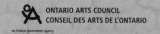

The publisher gratefully acknowledges the support of the Canada Council for the Arts and the Ontario Arts Council for its publishing progra
We acknowledge the financial support of the Government of Canada through the Canada Book Fund (CBF) for our publishing activities.

Library and Archives Canada Cataloguing in Publication

Heras, Theo, author
Hat on, hat off / by Theo Heras ; illustrations by Renné Benoit.
ISBN 978-1-927485-34-7 (hardcover)
I. Benoit, Renné, illustrator II. Title.
PS8615.E687H38 2016   jC813'.6   C2016-901086-4

Publisher Cataloging-in-Publication Data (U.S.)

Names: Heras, Theo, author. | Benoit, Renné, illustrator.
Title: Hat on, hat off / Theo Heras ; Renné Benoit.
Description: Toronto, Ontario Canada : Pajama Press, 2016. | Summary: "Baby is getting dressed to go out. But as often as his big sister add
new piece of clothing, he tosses his hat aside"— Provided by publisher.
Identifiers: ISBN 978-1-92748-534-7 (hardcover
Subjects: LCSH: Hats – Juvenile fiction. | Clothing and dress – Juvenile fiction. | Brothers and sisters – Juvenile fiction. | Undressing – Juve
fiction. | BISAC: JUVENILE FICTION / Clothing & Dress. | JUVENILE FICTION / Family / Siblings. | JUVENILE FICTION / Health
Daily Living / Daily Activities.
Classification: LCC PZ7.H473Hat | DDC [E] – dc23

Original art created in watercolour and digital
Designed by Rebecca Bender

Manufactured by Sheck Wah Tong Printing Ltd.
Printed in Hong Kong, China

Pajama Press Inc.
181 Carlaw Ave. Suite 207 Toronto, Ontario Canada, M4M 2S1

Distributed in Canada by UTP Distribution
5201 Dufferin Street Toronto, Ontario Canada, M3H 5T8

Distributed in the U.S. by Ingram Publisher Services
1 Ingram Blvd. La Vergne, TN 37086, USA

To Patrick Lester Stokes
—TH
For Emmett and Amelia
—R.B.

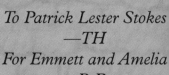